~ For Dorothy Harvey

WANTED

THE VOLE BROTHERS

Two small, ravenous rodents
recently arrived from the country.
Last seen chomping and chewing
on daisies, tulips and roses.

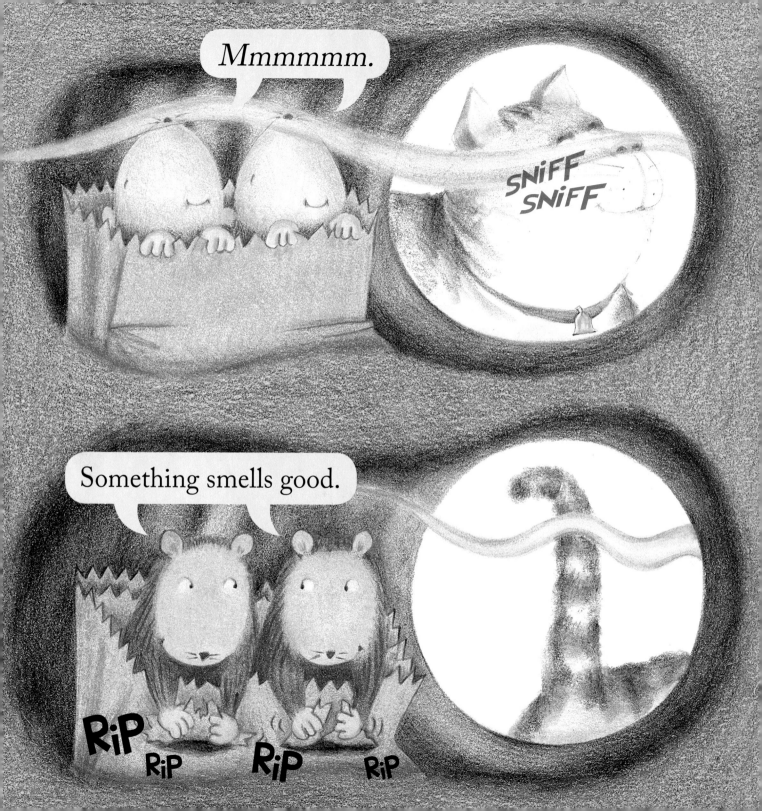

Quick.

Follow that cat!

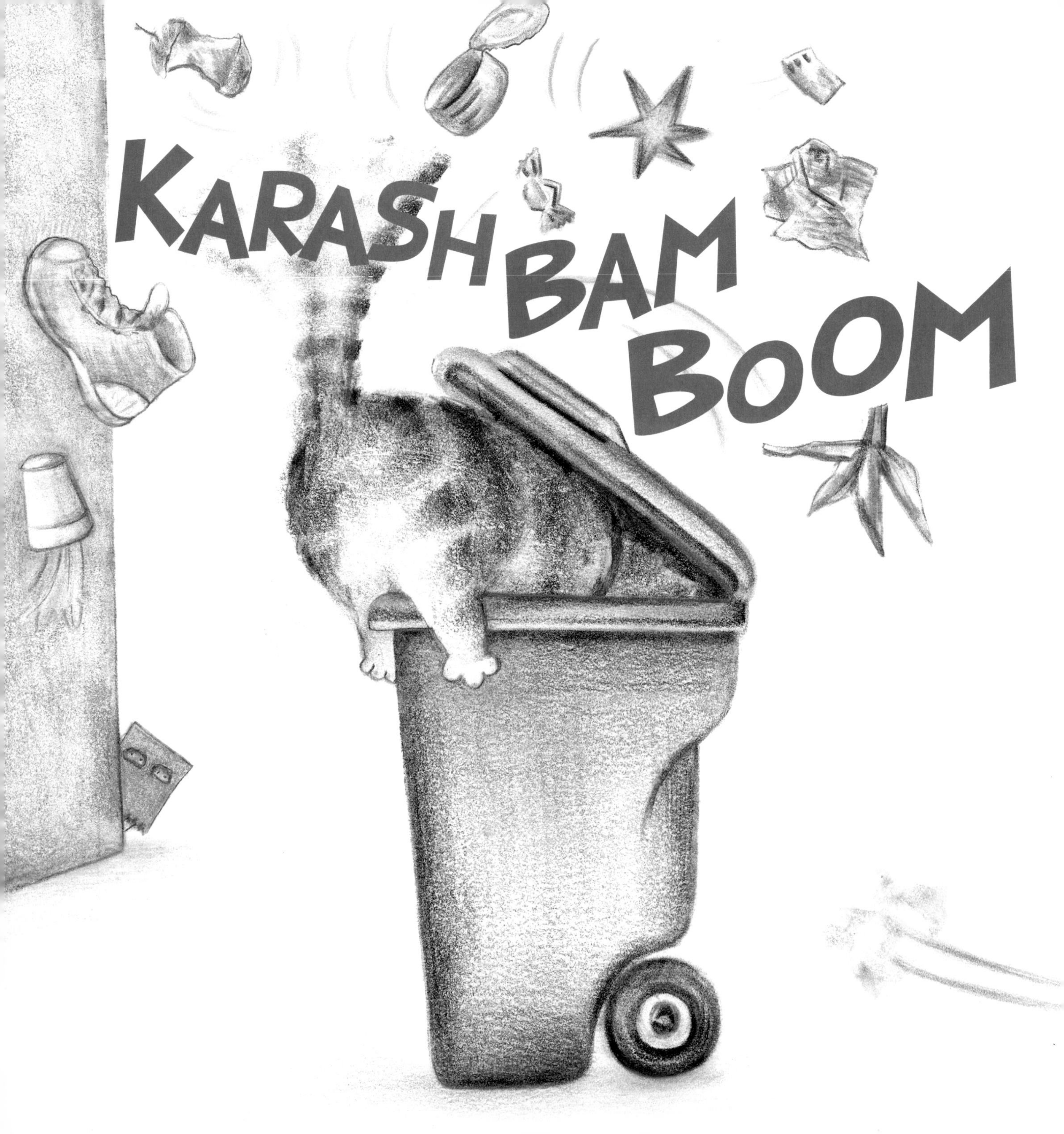
KARASH
BAM
BOOM

CAW
CAW

No, HE did.
HE took the pepperoni.

BEEP
BEEP

Oh, no!

Come back.
That's OUR pizza!

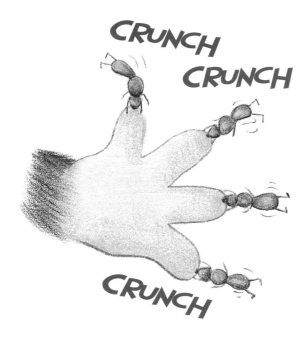

CRUNCH
CRUNCH

CRUNCH

OUCH!

They bit me.

Maybe they're hungry...

NOSH NOSH

...I'm starving.

BZZZZzz

Everyone's eating but us.

SLURP SLURP

GOBBLE GOBBLE

Oh, boy!

FLAP FLAP FLAP FLAP FLAP

Owlkids Books Inc.
10 Lower Spadina Avenue, Suite 400, Toronto, Ontario M5V 2Z2
www.owlkids.com

Library and Archives Canada Cataloguing in Publication

Schwartz, Roslyn, 1951-
       The vole brothers / Roslyn Schwartz.

Issued also in electronic format.
ISBN 978-1-926818-83-2

       I. Title.

PS8587.C5785V65 2011   jC813'.54   C2011-900237-X

Library of Congress Control Number: 2010943317

E-book ISBN: 978-1-926818-84-9

Canada Council   Conseil des Arts
for the Arts   du Canada

ONTARIO ARTS COUNCIL
CONSEIL DES ARTS DE L'ONTARIO

We acknowledge the financial support of the Canada Council for
the Arts, the Ontario Arts Council, the Government of Canada
through the Canada Book Fund (CBF), and the Government of
Ontario through the Ontario Media Development Corporation's
Book Initiative for our publishing activities.

Manufactured by WKT Co. Ltd.
Manufactured in Shenzhen, Guangdong, China in March 2011
Job #10CB4085

A   B   C   D   E   F

OWL kids   Publisher of Chirp, chickaDEE and OWL
www.owlkids.com

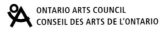

Now I'm full.

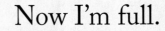

Me, too.

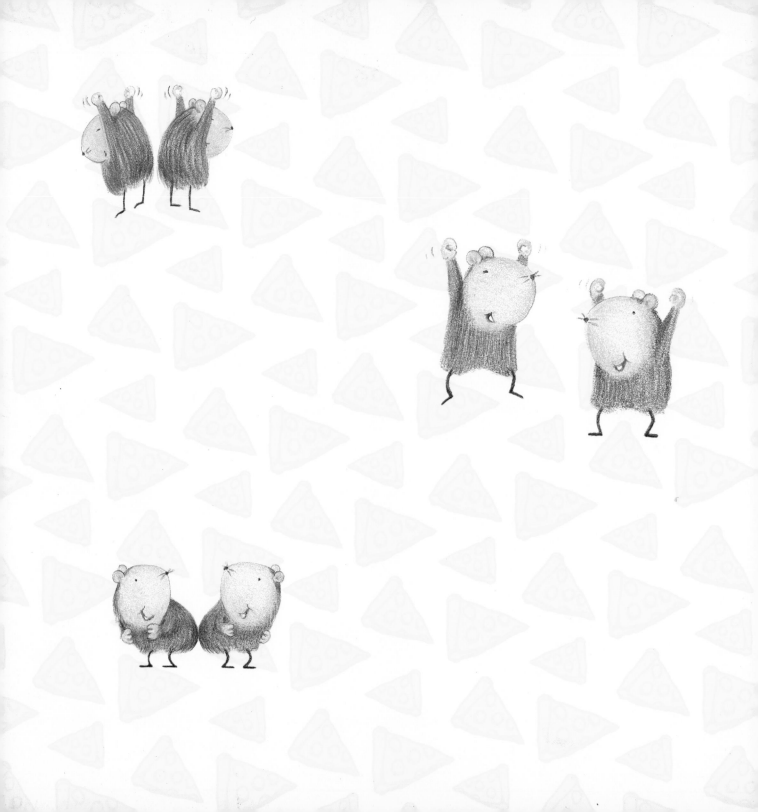